Geraldine's Baby Brother

by HOLLY KELLER

Greenwillow Books, New York

JP

For Radha
and Raghu,
with love

Watercolor paints and a black pen were used for the full-color art.
The text type is Times New Roman.

Printed in Hong Kong by South China
Printing Company (1988) Ltd.

First Edition   10 9 8 7 6 5 4 3 2 1

LIBRARY OF CONGRESS CATALOGING-IN-PUBLICATION DATA
Keller, Holly.
Geraldine's baby brother / by Holly Keller.
p.   cm.
Summary: Geraldine resents all the attention her
baby brother gets, until she spends some time with him.
ISBN 0-688-12005-9 (trade).   ISBN 0-688-12006-7 (lib. bdg.)
[1. Babies—Fiction.   2. Brothers and sisters—Fiction.]
I. Title.   PZ7.K28132Gc   1994
[E]—dc20
93-34491   CIP   AC

BHB

Geraldine put on her earmuffs
and sat behind the big chair.

"Why are you wearing earmuffs in the house?"
Uncle Albert asked when he saw her.
"So I can't hear *it*," Geraldine snapped, and
she pointed to Willie's basket.

"But I thought you wanted a baby brother,"
  Uncle Albert said.
"Not *that* one," Geraldine grumbled, and she
  turned the page without looking up.

The doorbell rang and Willie started to cry.
Mama came out of the kitchen.

Aunt Bessie came down from the bedroom,
and Papa got up from the sofa.

It was Mrs. Wilson to see Mama.
She had a big present for Willie
and a present for Geraldine, too.

"And where *is* Geraldine?" Mrs. Wilson asked while she was tickling Willie.

"Nowhere," Geraldine snarled from behind the chair.

So Mrs. Wilson left Geraldine's present on the table.

Willie cried
all morning.
Aunt Bessie
picked him up
and patted him.

Mama gave him a bottle,

and Papa carried
him all around
the house.

Uncle Albert made funny faces.

But at lunchtime Willie was still crying.

"Oh, dear," Mama said suddenly.

"Where's Geraldine? She must be starving."

Geraldine was in her room.
"How about a sandwich?" asked Mama.
Geraldine turned away. "I don't see you."

Mama sat down on the edge of the bed,
but Geraldine slid off the other side and
walked out the door.

Late in the afternoon Geraldine came into the kitchen. "I'm going to take my bath now, and then I'm going to bed."

"That's nice, dear," Mama said quickly over her shoulder. Willie was still screaming.

Papa was waiting outside the bathroom when
Geraldine opened the door.
"Aunt Bessie made lasagna for dinner, Geraldine,
especially for you."
"Not hungry," Geraldine grumbled, and she
disappeared into her room.

In the middle of the night Geraldine heard Willie moving around in his basket. She got out of bed and marched across the hall to the nursery.

"No more crying," she said sternly. Willie looked at her and yawned.
"I mean it," she added.

Willie rubbed his face
and stuck out his tongue.
"You're weird," she said.

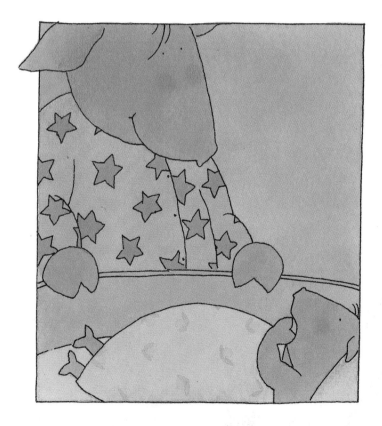

Willie stuffed his hand into
his mouth and sneezed,
and Geraldine laughed
because she couldn't help it.
But Willie didn't cry.

Geraldine stuck her fingers in her ears,
and he still didn't cry.

She turned on the light, and Willie gurgled.
So she sat in the rocking chair and read him some stories.

In the morning Mama found them both asleep.
"Breakfast, anyone?" she whispered.

Geraldine opened her eyes. She was *really* hungry. "Can I give Willie his bottle?" she asked, and she patted Willie's head.

"How nice," Mama said. "Can I give you a hug?"
"Soon," Geraldine answered, and she went
  downstairs for breakfast.